Alien

by

Tony Bradman

Illustrated by Harriet Buckley

First published in 2006 in Great Britain by
Barrington Stoke Ltd
18 Walker St, Edinburgh, EH3 7LP

www.barringtonstoke.co.uk

Reprinted 2007

ISBN: 978-1-84299-382-8

Printed in Great Britain by Bell & Bain Ltd

A Note from the Author

I love science fiction and war stories. Best of all are science fiction stories that are *about* wars – tales of alien invasions and humans who fight back, or battles in space. So I thought it would be fun to write a story like that.

I love science fiction films too – I'm a big fan of movies like *Terminator, Alien, Starship Troopers* and *War of the Worlds*. So when I started to think about this story I had lots of pictures in my head.

I like war stories but, in lots of ways this is an *anti*-war story. Most wars are stupid and go on long after people have forgotten why they started. I wanted to write a story where young people understand that, and *do* something about it. I hope you have as much fun reading it as I did writing it!

For Tom, who loves this kind of stuff
– just like me!

Contents

Chapter 1
Dead Kids

It was dark, but there was a moon. The ruins in front of them glowed blue. Jake raised his hand to halt his squad of fighters.

The glow can mean only one thing, he thought. *Krell weapons have been used*

here, and not long ago. Alien eyes may be fixed on the squad right now, alien fingers on triggers.

"Fan out and take cover," Jake said in a low voice. "Tiny, you're with me!"

Jake ducked behind a wall and watched the squad following his orders quickly and without a sound. Ten hard soldiers in helmets and body armour, their faces painted green and black. His squad, ready to fight even when they were worn out.

Not bad for a bunch of kids, thought Jake. *But then I'm just a kid too.*

"Shall I log on, Jake?" said Tiny, squatting down beside him.

Jake looked at his Comms Man. His real name was Gary, but the squad called him Tiny because he was so big. The battered old laptop Tiny pulled from his backpack seemed like a toy in his hands. Not many kids made it to Tiny's size by the time they were 12. *Not many kids make it to the age of 12 at all these days*, thought Jake. *I'm the oldest. How the heck did I make it to 14? Most of the squad are ten or 11. One of them is only nine.*

"Yeah, Tiny," Jake sighed. "Time for another little chat with HQ."

Tiny's fingers clicked over the laptop's keys, inputting the security code and their squad number. A face came up on screen, an old man with silver hair and cold blue eyes.

"Report, Squad Leader," said the man. "What's going on out there?"

"It looks like the enemy have been up to something in Sector 3, sir," said Jake. "Can I call in extra troops?"

"No, you can't," snapped the old man. "You must attack."

"But sir, we don't know how strong the enemy force is," said Jake. "And we're very tired. We've been on patrol for days now ..."

"We're all tired," said the old man. "But this is a war for the survival of the human race. You can rest when we've won. Is that clear?"

"Quite clear, sir," Jake said with a shrug, and gave the salute.

"Just do your job, Squad Leader," said the old man. "Over and out."

Tiny logged off, and closed the laptop. He looked at Jake and waited.

I know what he's thinking, thought Jake.
*He's hoping I won't obey orders, that I'll tell
the squad to pull back while we still can.
That's what I should do. I've seen too much
blood, too many dead kids. It's OK for The
Old Ones. They sit safe in their deep
bunkers while us kids do the dying. I'd give
anything to save the kids in my squad. But
how can I?*

"So what's the plan, Jake?" said Tiny.
"What are we going to do?"

"We don't have a choice, Tiny," said Jake. "We're going to attack."

Chapter 2
Feeling Jumpy

Jake called the squad over. They huddled round him in the moonlight, their eyes white in their dark faces.

"OK, listen up, guys," said Jake. "Same as usual. Katie, Shofiq and Joe, you take the right flank. Sarah, Dan and Alfie, you're on the left. Maria, Polly and Wicksy, you're in the middle with Tiny."

"Any idea how many Krell are in there?" said Sarah.

Good question, Sarah, thought Jake. *She'll make Squad Leader one day. After I'm dead ...*

"Could be just a patrol, like us," Jake said. "Could be more. The only way we'll find out is by going in."

"The more the merrier," said Alfie. He checked the energy level in his rifle and grinned. "Bring on the whole Krell army, that's what I say."

The others laughed. *They're feeling jumpy*, thought Jake. *They know that what lies ahead might be pain and death and some of them not coming back. But they'll follow me if I ask them.*

"And what about you, Jake?" Tiny asked. "Where will you be?"

"Out front, as ever," said Jake. "It's a tough job, but someone's got to do it." One or two of them began to laugh again. But not all of them.

"OK, people," Jake said. "Let's go to work. And stay cool."

"Yeah, and you take it easy too, Jake," said Tiny. Their eyes met.

"I'll be fine, Tiny," said Jake, smiling. "Don't you worry about me."

Jake pulled down his helmet over his face ... and left the cover of the wall. He ran across open ground, keeping low. He made for a big ruin, his laser rifle up and ready. The squad fanned out on either side and behind him. He reached the ruin and went round it.

There was more open space beyond. Jake saw it was a playground. So the ruin must have been a school once ...

That's where we should be, thought Jake. *In a class learning stuff, or out playing games. I can't remember being at school. I was only there for a year before the Krell came and the Dark Time started. I had a Mum and Dad then, a brother and sister ...*

Jake slipped into a shadow. His mind filled with memories – bad things happening, hiding out alone, being found and trained to fight back.

The Old Ones always say they have to use kids, he thought. *Almost all the adults who could fight are dead by now. I wonder how the war started in the first place, why the Krell came here. Are they as evil as The Old Ones say? This can't go on much longer. Soon there won't be any kids left ...*

"Jake, watch out!" Tiny yelled suddenly. "They're behind you!"

There was a blue flash, and Jake felt a burning pain in his arm.

Chapter 3
Ambush!

Jake spun round and dived behind the nearest pile of rubble. *Oh no,* he thought. *I must have led us into an ambush after all.*

The dark night was filled with crackling laser beams, blue from the Krell, white from his squad. There were screams and yells, human and alien. Jake checked his arm. He had been hit. His sleeve was smoking where the Krell beam had ripped through it, and he was bleeding. But it didn't look like he'd been too badly hurt.

I don't have time to worry about it, he thought. *I can use the arm, and that means I can still fight.* He peered past the rubble ... and a blue beam blasted into it, spraying his face with dust and grit. He pulled back and lay flat for a second, while he got his breath back. Then he rolled to the other side of the rubble and looked out again. He was more careful this time.

There was no blue beam. The Krell fire was aimed at his squad now. *They're being squeezed hard from both flanks*, Jake thought.

Suddenly he went cold all over. Somehow the Krell had got between him and the squad. He was cut off and quite on his own. So that meant the Krell could take him out whenever they wanted.

Not if I can help it, thought Jake. *I'll have to go further into the ruins.*

Then maybe I can work my way around, join up with the squad again. I hope no one else has been hit yet ...

Jake crawled away from the rubble into deeper shadow. He looked back across the playground. The fire-fight seemed to be getting worse. *There's nothing else I can do,* he thought. *I'll have to stick to my plan.*

He turned and ran out of the playground, keeping low. Dark shapes loomed up around him. *Just the same old burnt-out cars and ruins,* he thought. *So why does it feel spookier than normal? Maybe lots of people died here. Maybe their ghosts are watching me ...* He stopped to think which way he should go. *Left or right? It doesn't really matter.*

It was oddly still away from the fire-fight, too. So still that he could hear footsteps ... Jake froze. The hairs prickled on the back of his neck.

I'm being followed, he thought. *The Krell must have spotted me.*

Jake jumped over a low wall and hid behind it. He scanned the darkness, for any sign of movement, or the glow of an alien weapon. *Wait* ... he thought. *Is that something, or are my eyes just playing tricks?*

Suddenly a blue beam shot out of the night and sizzled past Jake's ear. He fired back, but another blue beam blasted into the top of the wall, then another. Jake turned and fled, looking for more cover.

He could hear footsteps in the ruins behind him.

Chapter 4
Cornered!

Jake ran. He slipped and stumbled. His arm was starting to hurt much more, and he could feel warm blood trickling down inside his sleeve. Soon his breath was coming in gasps. He didn't think he could keep going.

He stopped by the stump of a lamp-post. A blue blast sizzled into it.

Damn, he thought. *They're getting too close.* He looked round in despair. He saw a house nearby, its door open. *Got to hide,* he thought and, ducked inside. *Maybe they'll go past and I can go back the way I came ...* But the hall was blocked with rubble. The stairs were his only way to a hiding place.

Jake took them two at a time ... then tripped at the top and fell on the arm that had been shot. He cried out with pain and

dropped his rifle. He felt for it in the dark

– but he heard footsteps in the street, and

froze for a second. There was silence …

then the footsteps came closer. Jake

dragged himself into one of the rooms as

silently as he could.

There was a big hole where a window

had been. Moonlight was pouring in,

leaving only the corners of the room in the

dark. Jake crawled over to a corner far

from the door and sat there, his back

against the wall. *I'm trapped*, he thought.
But I won't die without a fight.

He pulled out his combat knife. Pain
shot down his arm, and he winced.

He listened, aware of every sound. And
there were the footsteps again.

Inside the house now, thought Jake.
*They're checking it out ... maybe they'll just
take a quick look round and move on.
Maybe they'll think I kept running.* A stair
creaked, a second, a third. *No such luck,*

thought Jake. He gripped the hilt of his

knife. *Here they come ...*

The footsteps were on the landing. Jake

pulled himself to his feet as a dark shape

filled the doorway. It was a Krell warrior.

The moonlight glinted on the alien body

armour and weapon. Krell helmets always

hid their faces. *I'm glad about that,* he

thought. *I don't want the last thing I ever*

see to be a look of hate ...

Jake raised his knife and got ready to

attack, his body tense, his eyes fixed on the

alien's weapon. The alien seemed to take aim, and Jake waited for the blue flash, the agony as the laser beam sliced and diced him. But nothing happened. The warrior stood there silent, and still. Jake suddenly felt very angry.

"Come on, you alien monster!" he yelled. "Give it your best shot!"

Then the alien did something Jake wasn't expecting. It dropped the gun to the floor with a clatter. It unsealed its helmet with a hiss and slowly took it off.

Jake stared at a pair of soft, golden eyes.

"No, human," said the alien. "I've seen too much death already."

Chapter 5
A Huge Trick

Jake dropped his knife. He had been told
by The Old Ones to hate the Krell, to think
of them as evil. But in all these years of
fighting, he had never been this close to an
alien. Not a living one, anyway.

I was never sure they were evil, he thought. *I know we've done just as many bad things in this war. And that face – two eyes, a nose, a mouth ... it's not much different from mine. She looks the same age as me. And she must be a girl. She couldn't be anything else with eyes like that.*

"So what now?" Jake said. "Are you letting me go?"

"If that is what you want," said the alien. Her voice was gentle, with a soft lilt to it. "But perhaps we could ... talk a little."

"What is there to talk about?" Jake said. *This is unreal*, he thought. *Am I dreaming? No, I can't be. The pain in my arm is far too real for that.*

"This stupid war," said the alien. She walked over to the window. Jake backed off, still nervous of her. "I saw you running in the ruins," she said, "and I knew it was my duty to kill you. But I could not do it. I looked at you and I ... I wanted to know your name."

"My name?" said Jake, surprised. "Er ... it's Jake. What's yours?"

"I am Tala," she said. "Squad Leader of the Krell Night Scouts."

"I'm a Squad Leader too," said Jake. He almost told her the number of his unit, but then he stopped himself. *Maybe this is a set-up*, he thought. *Maybe it's just a cunning way to find out more about us. But there's something about her. Something open ...*

"I see you do not trust me yet," said Tala. "I do not blame you. There are many among the Krell who would find it hard to trust a human."

"But not you," said Jake, moving closer to her. "And you're spot on about this war. It is stupid. I don't even know how it started. Do you?"

Tala gave a sigh and looked out of the window. Jake did the same. Ruins stretched as far as they could see beneath the silver moonlight. Some patches still glowed blue. Far off the fire-fight went on. Laser beams flickered and sizzled.

"The Elders say our planet was dying, and that we came here to seek help," Tala said. "They say you made us welcome at first, but then some of you turned on us, and we fought back. They say that this is a fight for our survival. That you want to wipe us from your planet."

"Hey, that's what our Old Ones say too," said Jake. The pain in his arm was very bad now, and he was starting to feel hot and dizzy. "And I'll bet the only people doing the fighting on your side are the kids. It's all a huge trick, isn't it, Tala?"

Jake wanted to say a lot more, but the room seemed to be spinning. *I'm passing out,* he thought. Then his mind went dark and he fell ...

Chapter 6
Healing Time

He woke to find Tala kneeling beside him. She pressed a metal disc against his wound. There was a blue glow, and Jake felt a wonderful wave of coolness spread up through his arm and into the rest of his body.

"There, the medicine works on you," Tala said. "Our flesh is not so alien to each other. But you will still need some healing time."

Tala helped him up. He shook his head, took some deep breaths.

"Healing time ..." he said. "We could all do with some of that, Tala. Both sides, human and Krell. But first we need to stop the killing."

"Yes, but how?" said Tala. "We are children. The Elders will not listen to me. And they have much in common with your Old Ones."

"They won't live forever, though, will they?" said Jake, suddenly smiling. "And for now we can both tell the others. I'll tell my squad what you've told me. And you can tell your warriors that there are humans the Krell can trust. The truth will make it harder for us to kill each other."

Maybe I will be able to save the kids in my squad, thought Jake, *and many more like them. The only winner in a war like this is Death.*

"It is a good plan, Jake," said Tala, smiling. "A good plan indeed."

Jake smiled too, then held out his hand. Tala removed her glove, and took it. Jake could feel her skin smooth against his blood-stained palm.

"I must get back to my squad," said Jake. "Are they OK?"

"They are good fighters, Jake," said Tala. "They are fine." Jake moved towards the doorway, but Tala gently held his arm. "Wait," she said. "I must give the signal." She moved to the landing and called out softly in her own language.

It sounds like a waterfall, thought Jake. *I wish I could speak her language as well as she speaks mine. Maybe one day I will.*

Outside in the street Jake saw why Tala had stopped him going first. Two more Krell warriors stepped silently from the shadows. *She could have come in with back-up,* thought Jake. *I wouldn't have stood a chance.*

"So we have both learned something today, Jake," said Tala.

"You're right," said Jake. "Take care of yourself, Tala."

"I will, Jake," she said. "And you take care of yourself, too."

Just then Jake heard something behind him in the ruins. He looked round and saw people running their way, heard human voices.

"Hey, you'd ..." he said, turning to tell Tala and her warriors that they had better leave fast. But they had already slipped into the darkness.

"Jake, something crazy is going on," Tiny said, running up, the rest of the squad following. "The Krell had us pinned down, but suddenly they just vanished. Listen, I'm sorry we lost you. Are you OK?"

"Sure, Tiny," said Jake. "Come on, let's get back to HQ."

He had an awful lot to do, and the time to start was now.

Barrington Stoke would like to thank all its readers for commenting on the manuscript before publication and in particular:

Eddie Calvert

Allison Conlin

Phillip Cornwall

Lauren Gibbon

Declan Hughes

Ugesh Jeganathan

Ryan Leckie

Christopher Marshall

Mhairi McNelig

Iain Petrie

Ryan Pinnington

Paul Smith

Joel Stanley

Jane Wainwright

Become a Consultant!

Would you like to give us feedback on our titles before they are published? Contact us at the address below – we'd love to hear from you!

Email: info@barringtonstoke.co.uk
Website: www.barringtonstoke.co.uk

If you loved this book, why don't you read ...

Speed
by Alison Prince

THE NEED FOR SPEED

Deb loves to drive fast.

The faster, the better.

Until she goes too far, too fast ...

gr8reads

You can order *Speed* directly from our website at
www.barringtonstoke.co.uk

If you loved this book, why don't you read …

Stray
by David Belbin

EVEN IN A GANG, SHE'S ON HER OWN

Stray's in with the wrong lot.

Can Kev save her?

Or will she drag him down?

gr8reads

You can order **Stray** directly from our website at
www.barringtonstoke.co.uk

If you loved this book, why don't you read ...

Fight
by Chris Powling

MY MATE COULD TAKE YOU

Matt's mate is a big, tough guy.

So that must make Matt hard, too ...

Or does it?

gr8reads

You can order *Fight* directly from our website at
www.barringtonstoke.co.uk